LEGENDS OF CHIMA

LEGO CHiMA

ORIGINS:
A STARTER HANDBOOK

by Tracey West

SCHOLASTIC INC.

ISBN 978-0-545-51652-5

12 11 10 9 8 7 6 5 4 3 2 1   13 14 15 16 17 18/0

Printed in the U.S.A.   40

First printing, January 2013

CHAPTER ONE
THE GREAT STORY

Welcome to the land of Chima. Here, a powerful force called CHI flows freely. But it wasn't always this way. The Great Story tells how the CHI came to Chima . . . and changed things forever.

A THOUSAND YEARS AGO, THE LAND OF CHIMA WAS A PEACEFUL PLACE.

Lions stalked the wide-open plains. Gorillas lived in the leafy trees of the jungle. Eagles and ravens flew across the clear blue sky. Crocodiles swam in the rivers that flowed through the land. And wolves spied on them all from the safety of lush, green plants.

There were no buildings or cars or planes. The animals of Chima walked on all fours, and the birds flew through the clear skies. They lived a simple life in this beautiful land.

Then, one fateful day, everything changed.

On that day, the sky grew black with storm clouds. *Boom!* Thunder roared through the land. A monster lightning bolt shot down from the sky, hitting a river. The water began to swirl like a tornado, rising up into the sky. Beneath it, the ground opened up.

The animals watched, amazed. A beautiful mountain came up from deep inside the earth. It floated up into the sky. Then the mountain hovered over Chima. Some mysterious force was holding it in place.

TODAY, THE WARRIORS OF CHIMA CALL THIS MOUNTAIN MOUNT CAVORA.

Water began to flow down the sides of Mount Cavora from a great waterfall. It flowed down the mountain and into the river below.

But this was not ordinary water. **It was CHI.**

The CHI seemed to glow with all the colors of the rainbow. And it contained amazing powers. CHI was the source of life — and also the source of destruction. But the animals of Chima did not know this yet. Curious, they slowly gathered around the pool of CHI.

A lion was the first to taste the CHI. He strolled to the riverbank and sniffed the water. Then he took a sip — and something amazing happened.

The lion transformed into a new creature.

Now he stood on two legs. Instead of paws, he had hands that could grasp and build things. He looked around, seeing everything that surrounded him as if for the first time.

Other animals sipped from the pool. A crocodile. A gorilla. An eagle. A raven. A wolf. More and more animals drank. One by one, they transformed.

Mount Cavora transformed, too. The faces of

the new Chima creatures appeared on its rocky face.

The animals soon realized that the CHI had changed them in many ways. They were smarter and more complex. They could walk and talk. They could do things they had never even dreamed of before. A new age had dawned in Chima.

But not all of the animals drank from the pool of CHI. Some wanted to remain pure, so they slipped away into the dangerous Outlands. Today, the Chima warriors call them Legend Beasts. Ancient myths say that they will return to Chima when they are needed most. But none have been seen for a thousand years. Some warriors believe they don't really exist at all.

The animals that drank the CHI stayed behind. **They formed tribes: the Lions, the Eagles, the Wolves, the Gorillas, the Ravens, and the Crocodiles.** They learned how to harness the CHI and became great warriors.

For a thousand years they respected the power of the CHI. And they told the Great Story to all young warriors so they would never forget where they came from.

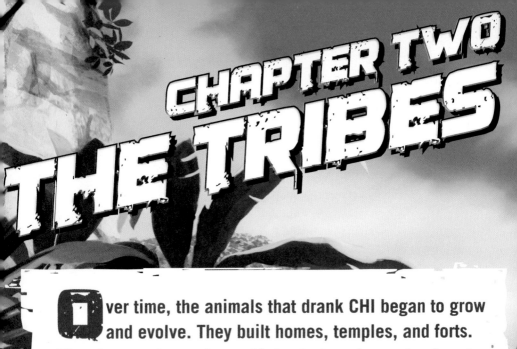

CHAPTER TWO
THE TRIBES

O ver time, the animals that drank CHI began to grow and evolve. They built homes, temples, and forts. They invented amazing vehicles to travel over land, water, and air. Their creations transformed Chima into a great and powerful land.

The animals also formed tribes based on their species. Each tribe lived in its own community. The tribes were different, but they all had one thing in common: the power of CHI.

THE LION TRIBE

The Sacred Pool of CHI is located in the Lion Temple. Special minerals in the pool combine with the CHI to form orbs. These orbs contain great power. The Lion Tribe distributes the orbs to the other tribes.

Why would the other tribes give the Lions such a great responsibility? It's probably because the Lions are known for being just and fair. They are very strict about following the rules in Chima. Without rules, the Lions believe, Chima will fall.

Members of the Lion Tribe are also known for their courage. They are experts at navigating hilly and rocky places. In battle, Lions combine their skill at working with CHI with their great physical strength in order to take down their opponents. Their fighting style has been compared to that of gladiators — bold and in-your-face.

LAVAL

Son of King LaGravis, Laval is the prince of the Lion Tribe. He knows that one day he will be called on to lead his tribe, and Laval really wants to live up to that responsibility.

But Laval is still a young Lion. He likes to have fun, and sometimes he'd rather be with his friends than attend to his duties in the Lion Temple. Laval also has a fiery streak to match his red mane. He'll often act without thinking, and if he's curious about something, he'll chase after it.

That means that Laval sometimes breaks the rules, which is a problem for a member of a rule-loving tribe like the Lions. If Laval is going to become a brave leader of his tribe, he's going to have to figure out how to follow the rules while staying true to his heart.

PERSONALITY:
Headstrong, loyal, and playful

FAVORITE ACTIVITY:
Playing hide-and-seek with his best friend, Cragger

QUOTE:
"I'd never sell out a friend."

KING CROMINUS

CRAGGER

THE CROCODILE TRIBE

Deep in the murky swamps of Chima you'll find the Crocodile Tribe. Their homes are partially under-water, because these warriors are just as comfortable in water as they are on land.

These swamp dwellers are as slippery as their environment, and sneaky, too. It's not safe to trust a Croc. They'll smile at you one minute and attack you the moment you turn your back.

If they attack, you'd better be on your game. Crocs are fierce fighters. Their super-tough skin protects them like armor, and they create weapons that resemble their own sharp fangs. Their fighting style has a lot of bite!

CRAGGER

If Crocs are fierce, then Cragger is the fiercest one of all. He's super-competitive and will do anything to win. The spinning blades of his Snaggle-Toothed Spear have sent many opponents running for cover. He has only been the leader of the Crocodile Tribe for a short time, but even his own tribe members shiver in fear when they see him.

Cragger wasn't always this way. Once, he knew how to have fun, and he was friends with all kinds of different creatures — including Laval, who was his best friend. But a series of events changed Cragger, and now he's the greatest threat to peace that Chima has ever faced.

CRAGGER

PERSONALITY:
Competitive, sly, and aggressive

FAVORITE ACTIVITY:
Plugging CHI

QUOTE:
"There's the CHI, ours for the taking!"

THE EAGLE TRIBE

Living in tall cliff dwellings, the Eagle Tribe has a unique view of Chima. But even though they live high above everyone else, they will still swoop in to help when Chima is in danger. The Eagles often come to the aid of their friends in the Lion Tribe.

Eagles are known to be observers and thinkers. While they're generally very smart, they're also known as "air-heads." They can be flighty and easily distracted. They love to talk and will happily spend hours discussing their favorite poem or battle strategy.

In battle, Eagle Warriors are known for their aerial assaults. They can attack at amazing speed and with powerful force. These masters of the sky can hold their own in any situation.

ERIS

Eris loves adventure and will always accept a challenge when it's handed to her. Like most Eagles, Eris is a great thinker who loves to solve puzzles and tell exciting stories. But she's not as much of an "airhead" as the rest of her tribe — she's very focused and stays calm when things get tough. That's probably why she's friends with earth-dwelling creatures like Laval.

Laval has found Eris to be his most loyal friend. She's always there when he needs her, and she'll never leave a friend behind when there's trouble.

When it's time to battle, Eris uses strategy to confuse and defeat her opponents. She's also a fast, skilled flyer who brings intensity and courage into every situation. Laval is thankful he has a warrior like Eris on his side.

ERIS

PERSONALITY:
Smart, adventurous,
and loyal

FAVORITE ACTIVITY:
Telling stories

QUOTE:
"Don't worry; I've got
an idea. . . ."

THE WOLF TRIBE

Like ninja, members of the Wolf Tribe are swift and silent, and often attack their opponents by surprise. They like to move under cover of darkness, and even their vehicles are camouflaged so you can't see them coming.

These warriors may be sneaky, but they're also ferocious fighters. To them there's no shame in running away from a fight if they're losing. Their goal is always to win, but if they can't do that, they'll retreat, regroup, and try again another day.

Wolves like to travel in packs, and they're always on the move. Their vehicles double as living quarters, but you won't find them decked out with the comforts of home. Their convoys are equipped with weapons so the Wolves are prepared for any situation.

The Crocodile Tribe can usually count on the Wolves to take their side, but they need to remember: Wolves don't really care about anyone or anything except their own tribe.

WORRIZ

Because they're always on the move, the Wolf Tribe is always meeting new tribes. They need a warrior to represent them to make sure they can pass through other territories without any trouble. Worriz is their go-to Wolf.

Did they choose him because he's so nice and friendly? Not exactly. Worriz is best at *pretending* that he's friendly. He's actually cruel and ruthless. But he can hide his true nature long enough to fool others. He can even be charming when he wants to be. Then, when he gets what he wants, he drops the act.

Like other wolves, Worriz has one main weakness — his nose. Yes, his excellent sense of smell can be a real help sometimes. But a bad smell — like a skunk, for example — will send him running away with his tail between his legs.

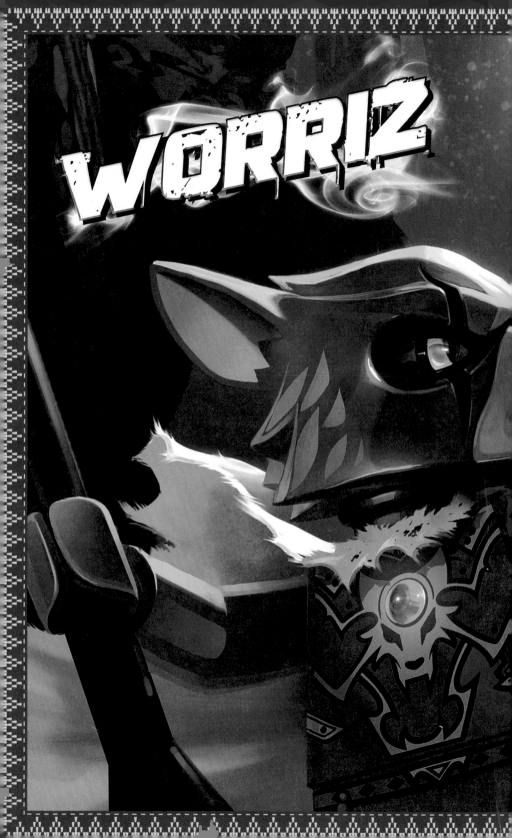

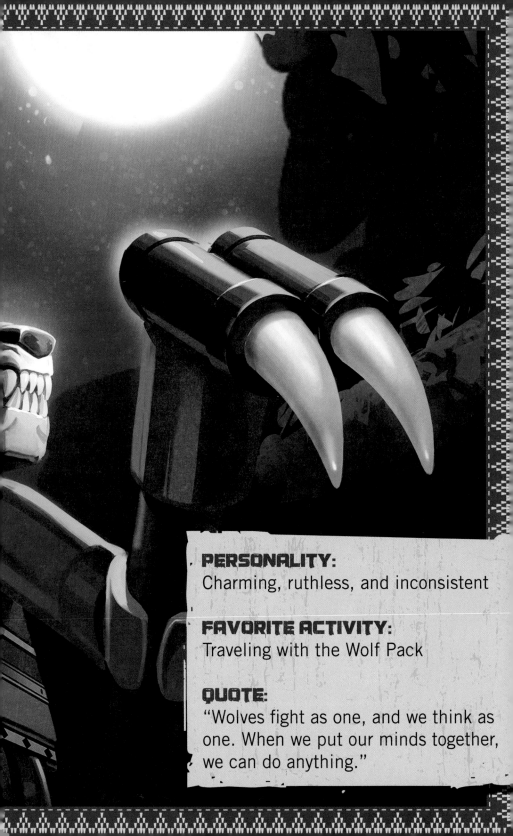

PERSONALITY:
Charming, ruthless, and inconsistent

FAVORITE ACTIVITY:
Traveling with the Wolf Pack

QUOTE:
"Wolves fight as one, and we think as one. When we put our minds together, we can do anything."

THE RAVEN TRIBE

Money, money, money — that's all Ravens seem to care about. They will lie, cheat, and steal to get what they want. They're extremely tricky, too. A Raven will take the armor off your back and then try to sell it back to you — for fifty percent off, because you're such a good friend.

Ravens build their forts out of the junk they steal and collect. These ramshackle nests may look messy, but they're surprisingly complicated. Anyone trying to sneak into a Raven Tribe fort will easily get lost in the maze's twists and turns.

Raven Warriors will go to battle if they're paid enough — or if they feel that their honor has been challenged. With their sharp, armored beaks and powerful wings, they can be vicious foes. Most creatures in Chima steer clear of the Ravens as best they can. It's simply the safest thing to do.

RAZAR

Razar is a typical Raven — greedy and selfish down to the tips of his wings. He'll steal anything that isn't tied down, and if it is tied down he'll steal a pair of scissors so he can cut the rope.

Razar has decided to side with Cragger in the battle for Chima, but it's nothing personal against the Lion Tribe. He thinks that he'll gain more riches in the end if he helps out the Crocs. He makes his decisions based on what he'll get out of a situation, and doesn't think about right or wrong.

If you ask Razar what his favorite things are, he'll tell you "trinkets and treasure," and that's true. But there's one thing he loves even better than gold — and that's himself!

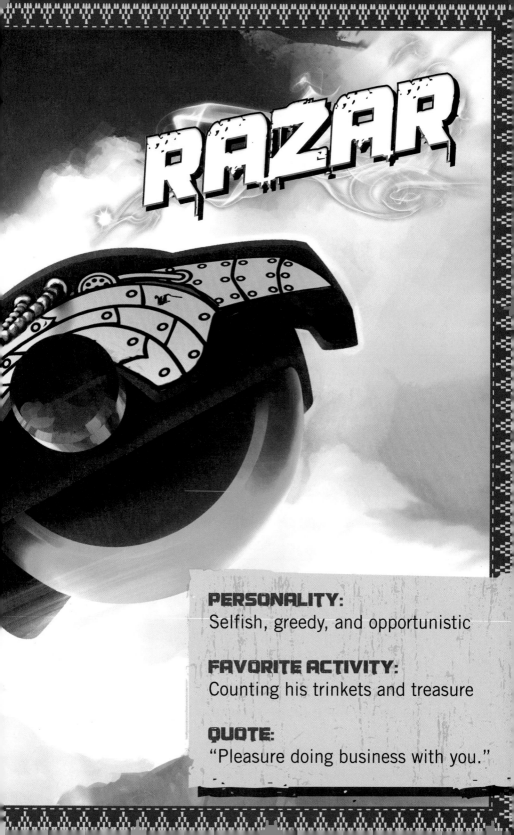

RAZAR

PERSONALITY:
Selfish, greedy, and opportunistic

FAVORITE ACTIVITY:
Counting his trinkets and treasure

QUOTE:
"Pleasure doing business with you."

CHAPTER THREE
GROWING UP IN CHIMA

Once, all the animal tribes lived together in peace. They worked together and played together. They gathered to enjoy contests of skill. Lions, Crocodiles, Eagles, Wolves, Gorillas, and Ravens were all friends with one another.

And then something happened to change all that — something that threatened to change Chima forever. How did the fighting begin? To learn the answer, we need to go back to a happier time. . . .

How did the trouble start in Chima? The seeds of conflict were planted a short while ago. . . .

"Cragger? Where are you?" Laval called out.

Laval walked along the banks of the lagoon, squinting. Could Cragger be underwater? That was a perfect place for a Crocodile to hide.

Then the young Lion saw a swift movement over by the Forever Rock. Slowly, quietly, Laval peeked behind it. . . .

"Aha!"

Cragger jumped out and tackled Laval. The two friends rolled across the grass, laughing.

LAVAL

"Hey, this game is called 'hide-and-seek,' not 'hide-and-attack,'" Laval protested.

"Oh, you and your rules. Don't you Lions ever want to improvise?" Cragger asked.

"Sure!" Laval replied. "In fact, we even have rules about improvising."

Cragger snorted. "Of course! More rules! What's this one called?"

"Banana," Laval replied.

Cragger looked confused. "Banana what?"

"Banana on the Crocodile's Tail," Laval answered.

"Huh?" Cragger looked behind him to see that Laval had tied a banana to his tail. The meaty hand of a Gorilla dropped down from the tree above them.

Gorzan the Gorilla grabbed the banana, pulling Cragger along with it.

"*Mmm*, munchies! Thanks, Crocodude!" Gorzan said.

"Put me down, Gorzan!" Cragger yelled.

Laval laughed. "That's another one for me, you mud-lover," he teased.

"Oh, go cough up a hairball, you overgrown cat," Cragger shot back. Then they both burst out laughing.

That's how it was with Laval and Cragger. They may have been born into different tribes, but they loved to play together. Both of them liked to explore. They loved to compete. And they were both very curious about CHI, the mysterious life-force that flowed from Mount Cavora. One day soon, they would be given CHI harnesses and allowed to create Orbs of CHI from the Sacred Pool. But not yet. They were still too young.

One day, the friends were having a mock duel. Panting, they rested against Forever Rock, looking out over Chima.

"Quick question: Who's your best friend?" Cragger asked.

"Quick answer: You are," Laval replied.

"Yes! Same here!" Cragger said with a grin.

"Isn't that obvious?" Laval asked. "Nothing will ever come between us."

Cragger nodded. "I know," he said. "Hey, you want to try something really awesome?"

Curious, Laval followed Cragger to the Lion Temple, a majestic stone structure in the heart of Lion territory. Inside was the Sacred Pool of CHI, where the CHI that flowed from the mountain was collected. Special salts in the pool caused the CHI to form into orbs. Wearing a CHI orb could give a warrior an amazing boost of power.

To Laval's surprise, Cragger began to climb up the rear wall of the Temple.

"Are you sure about this?" Laval asked. **"You're trying to sneak in to see the Sacred Pool of CHI?"**

"Don't you want to see it, too?" Cragger asked.

Laval nodded. "Well, yeah, we will. When we reach the Age of Becoming, we'll be able to plug CHI anytime we want."

"Come on," Cragger urged. **"There's no rule that says we can't look."**

Laval thought about it for a second, and then grinned. "Last one there's a rotten skunk!"

They scaled the wall and dropped down inside the Temple. A Lion Guard was pacing back and forth next to the pool. Laval's heart raced. What if they got caught?

But Cragger waited until the guard walked out of sight, and then ran to the edge of the pool. Laval followed him. They knelt down and gazed into the glowing blue water.

"Whoa. Will you look at that?" Cragger asked, mesmerized.

Laval looked around nervously, hoping the guard wouldn't return anytime soon. "Yeah, great. Seen it. Let's go."

When he turned back to his friend, Cragger was putting on a CHI harness. The Croc must have been secretly carrying it all along.

"What are you doing?" Laval hissed. "Stop that!"

"Haven't you always wanted to feel what it's like?" Cragger asked.

He reached into the pool. The

water formed a glowing Orb of CHI in his hand.

"Put that back! We can't! This is really bad!" Laval wailed.

"Ah, who's going to know?" Cragger asked. He put the Orb into the harness.

"Cragger, no!"

A surge of power rushed through Cragger's body. A glowing, ghostly image of his inner Power Warrior rose up behind him. Laval had seen this happen when warriors used CHI.

But something was wrong. Cragger's Power Warrior began to grow . . . and grow . . . and grow. He couldn't control it. Cragger floated up into the air.

"Cragger! Snap out of it!" Laval cried. He reached up, trying to pull down his friend.

Boom! Cragger's Power Warrior exploded, sending both friends flying across the temple. Lion Guards immediately surrounded them.

A guard bent down to see if Cragger was all right. The young Croc lifted his head and growled. The orb on his chest was glowing wildly. He charged forward, slamming into the guards. Then he leaped up and over the Temple wall.

"Cragger!" Laval yelled.

The young Crocodile had used the CHI before he could handle it. Panicked and full of energy, Cragger raced wildly through the land. Laval hopped onto his Speedor and tried to catch up to his friend.

Cragger crashed through bushes and tree branches as he tore a path toward Forever Rock. Laval finally caught up to him.

"Cragger, you have to calm — *aahhh!*"

Cragger spun around and tackled Laval. Suddenly, a blue pulse beam shot out of nowhere, striking Cragger. The Crocodile went flying back.

Laval looked up to see his father, King LaGravis, standing over them with two Lion Guards.

"Chain the Croc. Call his parents," LaGravis told his guards. Then he turned his attention to his son.

"What were you thinking? Sneaking into the Lion Temple? Taking CHI?" he growled.

LEONIDAS

"We just wanted a peek!" Laval replied. "I didn't know he was gonna plug in an Orb!"

LaGravis shook his shaggy head. "You're both too young for CHI! Look at what happens!" He nodded toward Cragger, who was trying to escape his heavy chains. "That's why we have these rules. Cragger could have really hurt himself. Or someone else."

Laval knew his father was right — he was the leader of the Lion Tribe, after all.

The guards took Cragger back to the Lion Temple. LaGravis and Laval followed them.

When they got there, three tough-looking Crocodile Tanks were parked outside. Inside, Cragger was out of his chains, and his father, King Crominus, was anxiously pacing the floor. His mother, Queen Crunket, stood nearby.

"How could you do this, LaGravis?" King Crominus asked angrily. **"Putting my son in chains?"**

"CHI-ing up before the Age of Becoming is strictly forbidden," LaGravis reminded him. "You know what happens."

"Yes, and so does your son," King Crominus snarled. "But that didn't stop him from making my Cragger plug CHI before his time."

"What? But I tried to stop him!" Laval protested.

"Quiet, Laval," his father warned.

The young Lion sat down next to his friend. He glared at Cragger.

"Hey, I had to tell him something," Cragger whispered.

Now the two tribe leaders faced each other.

"I believe an apology is in order," King Crominus said.

"Agreed," said LaGravis solemnly. "Then we can put this all behind us."

He turned and looked at Cragger. "So . . . about that apology. Whenever you're ready, Cragger."

"Actually, I was expecting an apology from you and your son," the Crocodile Leader said.

"What?" asked LaGravis.

Queen Crunket approached the two leaders. "You don't really think Cragger is to blame, do you? An impressionable young Croc . . . taken advantage of by a noble Lion, who should have known much better?"

"You've got to be kidding me!" Laval cried, jumping up. "It was all Cragger's idea!"

King Crominus stepped between Laval and the queen.

"Know your place, Lion Child," he warned.

LaGravis moved threateningly toward the Crocodile King.

"And you know yours," he growled.

King Crominus looked around the Temple, which was filled with Lion Guards.

"Perhaps we should settle this at another time . . . and another place," the Crocodile smoothly suggested.

"As far as I'm concerned, it is settled," LaGravis said. "For a

thousand years, the Lions have watched over this Pool of CHI. We ensure it is used properly by all in Chima. What your son did was not proper."

King Crominus shook his head. "Worst apology ever, LaGravis. This isn't over, Lions. We Crocodiles never forget. Ever."

The king marched out of the Temple. Queen Crunket and Cragger followed him.

"I thought it was elephants that never forget," Laval mumbled.

LaGravis sighed. "Laval, just go to your room."

"But I was playing with Cragger!" Laval protested.

His father's face was stern. "You won't be playing with Cragger ever again!"

KING CROMINUS

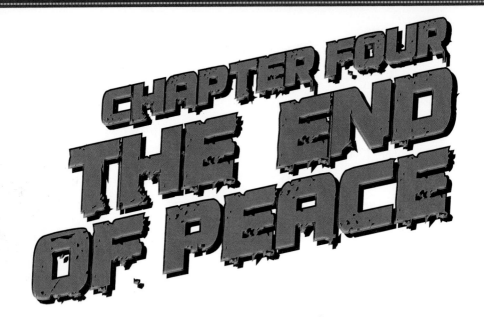

CHAPTER FOUR
THE END OF PEACE

Cragger's theft of CHI was just the beginning of the conflict. Things were tense between the Lion Tribe and Crocodile Tribe . . . and then something happened that would change Chima forever.

In the swamps of Chima, the green grass blew lazily in the breeze. A snaggletoothed blade sliced through the air, taking a chunk of grass with it. Cragger grinned triumphantly.

"Gotcha!" he cried.

His friend Worriz rose up from the grass with a sigh.

"Okay, you found me," he said. "Can we play something else now? Hide-and-seek is so . . ." He finished his sentence with a yawn.

"I know," Cragger agreed. "It's Laval's game. I'm much more into . . . hide-and-attack!"

He tackled Worriz playfully, but the Wolf just pushed him off. "Why don't you go see if Laval wants to play your kiddie games?"

"My father won't let me play with the Lions anymore," Cragger replied.

"Yeah, I heard," Worriz said. **"Plugging CHI before the Age? That's bold."**

"Thanks," Cragger said.

"I only have one question," Worriz said. "The CHI — what's it like?"

WORRIZ

A smile slowly crossed Cragger's face as he remembered. **"It's the best thing ever," he answered. "Like being born all over again, but with superpowers.** You just feel so strong. Like all of nature has crammed itself inside you, and it's just waiting to burst out."

Worriz hung on every word. Finally, Cragger was talking about something interesting.

LONGTOOTH

"Come on!" Cragger said. "I'll show you."

It was dark by the time they reached the Lion Temple. Cragger climbed up the rear wall, and Worriz followed him. They dropped down into the temple. The Sacred Pool of CHI glittered in the moonlight.

"Shouldn't there be more guards?" Worriz whispered.

"Who cares?" Cragger asked. "There's the CHI, ours for the taking!"

Cragger rushed to the pool. But a large Lion Sword crashed down in front of him.

Startled, Cragger looked up to see LaGravis flanked by two Lion Guards, Leonidas and Longtooth.

"It's not what you think," Cragger said nervously. "I was just . . . ask Worriz. He'll tell you."

But Worriz had already scrambled back over the wall.

Cragger quickly changed his story. "I mean, it was all Laval's idea."

Laval stepped out of the shadows. "Really? 'Cause I haven't been allowed out of my room in weeks. Just ask these guys here — they've been guarding it."

"Watch him while I call his father," LaGravis commanded.

"No! You can't do that!" Cragger cried, panicked.

"Yeah? And who's gonna stop us?" Longtooth asked menacingly.

Cragger whipped his tail around Longtooth's ankles. *Bam!* Longtooth hit the temple floor, face-first.

Leonidas lunged forward, but Cragger swung his tail again, and he went down, too. Cragger grabbed the guard's sword and swung it at LaGravis.

"Whoa! Cragger! Watch it!" LaGravis said, ducking.

Cragger ran away, and Laval tore after him.

"Hey, no one attacks my dad and gets away with it!" Laval yelled.

"Boys! Stop this, now!" LaGravis growled.

But they were over the wall before LaGravis could reach them.

Cragger jumped on his Speedor and zoomed off into the jungle. Laval did the same.

As he crashed through the trees, Cragger saw that Laval was only seconds behind him. He hesitated for a second, and then pulled out a small flare launcher. He fired it into the air, and a bright red light streaked across the sky.

Everyone in Chima knew what the signal meant. It was a call to war.

The guards in the Crocodile Fort saw it first.

"King Crominus! Come quick! It's the Croc-Flare!" cried Crug the guard.

LaGravis saw the flare from the Lion Temple.

"*Ughh.* Not good," he growled. "Leonidas! Longtooth! We need to prepare!"

Cragger had shot the flare over an area of Chima known as The Fangs. Jagged rocks rose up from the stony plain. Cragger hoped to lose Laval in the maze of rocks. But when he made his first turn, Laval was right there waiting for him.

"Laval? How'd you do that?" Cragger asked.

"My dad taught me how to ride up here at The Fangs," Laval explained. "There's no way you can outrun me in these rocks."

Cragger revved his Speedor and took off. He didn't get far before Laval cut him off again.

Cragger spun around and tried another way around the rocks, but Laval was waiting for him once more.

"What? Do you think I'm kidding?" Laval asked.

Cragger was frustrated. "Come on, we went everywhere together. How come you never took me up here?"

"Because it's dangerous!" Laval replied. "There are hidden sinkholes and caves all over The Fangs. That . . . and my dad has a rule against coming up here without him."

Cragger snorted. "Ugh. You and your rules again."

He gunned his Speedor, but his back wheel kicked up dirt, opening a small crack in the ground. His Speedor began to slide backward into the ever-growing hole.

Laval reached out a hand and grabbed him, pulling him to safety. The Speedor tumbled into a deep, dark cave.

"Watch it!" Laval warned. "That's a deep one. You know, sometimes it makes sense to follow a rule or two."

Cragger looked behind him at the hole. He was grateful to Laval for saving him — but not ready to be friends just yet.

"Thanks. But I can do without the lecture," Cragger

complained. **"You wanted to check out the Sacred Pool just as much as I did."**

"Yeah, for a little fun and adventure," Laval admitted. "But not for the CHI. "

Cragger got a dreamy look in his yellow eyes. "Oh, if only you knew what it felt like. The power! You'd do the same to me in a second."

Laval firmly shook his head. "No, Cragger, I wouldn't. **And I wouldn't sell out my best friend, either."**

The words *best friend* hit Cragger hard. For the first time, he felt bad about what he had done.

"Laval, I'm sorry about this," he said honestly.

"About what? The lying and backstabbing?" Laval shot back. "Or just breaking the rules and stealing CHI?"

"Actually, neither," Cragger admitted. "I'm sorry for calling them. . . ."

Three huge Croc Tanks rumbled into The Fangs, aiming their weapons at Laval. Several Croc Warriors sprang out and surrounded the young Lion.

Laval looked at Cragger in horror. "War tanks? Troops? Cragger, what have you done?"

"I panicked," Cragger admitted. "And I, uh . . . might have 'accidentally' sent up a Croc-Flare."

Laval's eyes blazed with anger. "You what?"

"Hey, I said I'm sorry," Cragger said. "Let me talk to them." He turned to the tanks. "Father?"

King Crominus and Queen Crunket stuck their heads out of the largest tank.

"Cragger, step away from the Lion," the king said.

"What?" Cragger was shocked.

CRAGGER

"We've been worried sick about you, darling," said the queen. "That Lion is a terrible influence!"

"But it's not his fault, Mother!" Cragger insisted. "Honestly, the Lions are okay!"

At that exact moment, three Lion Tanks roared onto the scene. The first accidentally hit one of the tall, twisting rock spires. The spire fell, crashing into the ground.

To the Crocs, it looked like an attack.

"Incoming!" shrieked one of the Croc Guards.

"Battle formations, everyone!" King Crominus cried, pulling the queen back into the tank.

"It's all a misunderstanding!" Cragger wailed. But one of the Croc Guards firmly pulled Cragger into another tank.

"We can't take that chance, son," King Crominus said.

Crug and Crawley, two Croc Warriors, clumsily tried to get their blasters ready. But the klutzy Crocs bumped into each other, accidentally triggering the blasters. Bright pulse beams shot across The Fangs, nearly hitting the Lion Tanks. Now the Lions thought the Crocs were firing on them.

"No hiding for you, LaGravis!" King Crominus yelled. "Fire the Clawpoon!"

Inside the tank, a Croc Guard loaded a massive harpoon with a claw on the end. The other guard pressed a button, firing the weapon.

The Clawpoon plunged deep into the side of LaGravis's tank. A strong metal line now connected the Croc Tank to the Lion Tank.

LaGravis realized his tank couldn't move. "Ugh. A Clawpoon? Really?"

King Crominus's tank slowly began to pull the Lion Tank backward. Leonidas sprang from the tank and tried to cut the cable, but a Croc Warrior whacked him with the side of a spear. Leonidas fell off the tank, and the two warriors battled on the ground.

Laval climbed onto his father's tank. **"Dad! We've got to stop this!"**

"Get down, Laval!" LaGravis warned. "That was a Croc-Flare they set up before. That only means one thing: full-on battle!"

"I know, but —"

BOOM! A blast from King Crominus's tank hit the Lion Tank, sending Laval flying.

"Laval!" LaGravis cried. Furious, he revved his tank, which was still linked to the Croc Tank. The Lion Tank's superpowered engine jerked the Croc Tank wildly, slamming it into a stand of rocks. Queen Crunket was thrown against the wall and caught her leg underneath a piece of twisted metal.

King Crominus had lost control of his vehicle. "Everybody out!" he yelled, and his Croc Guards quickly obeyed. Crominus ran to free his wife.

LaGravis continued to drag the Croc Tank, not realizing that he was heading toward the cave that Cragger's Speedor had opened up.

Cragger jumped out of his tank and ran toward the Lion Tank, waving his arms.

"Stop! The ground's unstable!" he yelled. "Please! This is all my fault! I shouldn't have taken the CHI! Or blamed Laval! Or shot that Croc-Flare. Blame me, not them!"

LaGravis stopped his tank, but it was too late. The Croc Tank was teetering on the edge of the hole. Still hurt, Laval got to his feet and limped up as quickly as he could.

"Dad! You've got to help them!" he cried.

His father stuck his head out of the tank. "I know. I'm trying to pull them toward more stable ground."

But Cragger thought that LaGravis was still trying to drag his parents into the hole. He rushed over to the Clawpoon cable and sliced it with his spear.

"What are you doing?" Laval asked, panicked.

The Croc Tank slid back toward the opening in the ground. The rock cracked underneath the tank treads, widening the hole.

"Noooooo!" Laval cried.

Cragger jumped onto the tank and tried to pry open the hatch, but it was stuck. From inside the tank, he heard his father's voice.

"You're in charge now, son."

"Make us proud," his mother added.

His father spoke again. "And whatever you do, don't —"

Before he could finish, the ground beneath completely crumbled and gave away.

"*Noooooooo!*" Cragger wailed. He stubbornly held on to the hatch, but Laval grabbed him by the tail, rescuing him just in time. The tank plummeted into the darkness.

Poor Cragger thought the worst had happened. Laval put a hand on his shoulder to comfort him. They didn't know that the tank had landed safely at the very bottom of the Gorge of Eternal Depth.

"Don't worry, my queen," King Crominus said, looking up at the daylight far above their heads. "We'll get out of here . . . eventually."

"But what about Cragger?" Queen Crunket asked.

"He knows the Lions are not to blame," her husband replied. **"He'll do the right thing. I was just trying to warn him: Whatever you do, don't listen to your sister. . . ."**

That night, Cragger sat sadly on the throne that once belonged to his father. He still couldn't believe that he was the leader of the Croc Tribe.

His sister, Crooler, sidled up to him. "Listen to me, brother," she said coldly. **"We'll make the Lions pay."**

"It wasn't the Lions' fault," Cragger said.

"Trust me," Crooler said. "They're our enemy, brother. Or should I say . . . King."

Cragger stared at the Crocodile Crown Helmet in his hands, unsure of what to do. Behind him, his sister gave a sly smile.

Cragger might be king, but Crooler knew her little brother would do whatever she wanted. **And what she wanted was a war with the Lions. . . .**

That is how it began. Now, sides have been chosen. Battles will be fought. And the friendship between Laval and Cragger will never be the same. . . .